Caring for Your Magical Pets

Taking Care of Your

Griffin

Eric Braun

BLACK
RABBIT
BOOKS

Hi Jinx is published by Black Rabbit Books
P.O. Box 3263, Mankato, Minnesota, 56002.
www.blackrabbitbooks.com

Marysa Storm, editor; Michael Sellner, designer;
Omay Ayres, photo researcher

Library of Congress Cataloging-in-Publication Data
Names: Braun, Eric, 1971- author, illustrator.
Title: Taking care of your griffin / by Eric Braun.
Description: Mankato, Minnesota : Black Rabbit Books, [2020] | Series: Hi Jinx. Caring for your magical pets | Summary: Provides easy-to-read instructions for choosing and caring for a pet griffin, as well as the difficulty of owning a meat-eating predator. Includes discussion questions. | Includes bibliographical references and index.
Identifiers: LCCN 2018042269 (print) | LCCN 2018052540 (ebook) | ISBN 9781680729177 (e-book) | ISBN 9781680729115 (library binding) | ISBN 9781644660904 (paperback)
Subjects: | CYAC: Griffins–Fiction. | Pets–Fiction.
Classification: LCC PZ7.1.B751542 (ebook) | LCC PZ7.1.B751542 Tan 2020 (print) | DDC [E]–dc23
LC record available at https://lccn.loc.gov/2018042269

Printed in China. 1/19

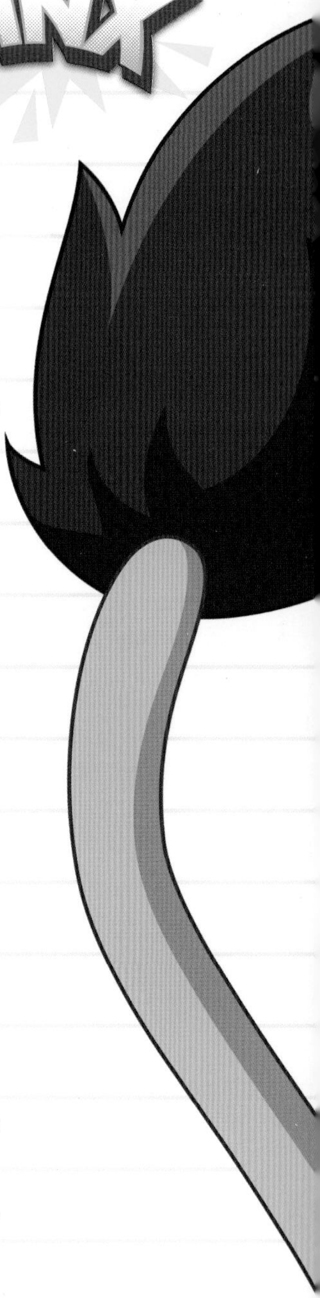

Image Credits

Dreamstime: Anna Velichkovsky, 1 (griffin), 12 (griffin); iStock: amdandy, 21 (griffin); jasonlean, 15 (r claws); Makort, 15 (kid), 23 (kid); rtisticco, 10–11 (bkgd); rubynurbaidi, 11 (griffin), 15 (btm griffin), 23 (griffin); Shutterstock: Alena Kozlova, 18–19 (hill); Aluna1, 8 (bkgd); Angeliki Vel, 9 (grass), 23 (grass); ChromaCo, 15 (r griffin head); Cory Thoman, Cover (griffin btm), 16 (griffin btm); Den Zorin, 4 (griffin); DVitaliy, 12 (barn); ekler, 17; GraphicsRF, Cover (grass), 16 (grass); Hengky Irawan, 8 (griffin); IQ Advertising, 4 (rabbit); maradon 333, 20 (fossil); mejnak, 16 (trees, clouds); Memo Angeles, Cover (griffin head, boy, chickens, bones), 1 (girl), 8 (boy), 9 (boy), 11 (chickens), 12 (griffin head, wings), 16 (griffin head, boy, chickens, pig), 18 (girl); Merggy, 4 (bkgd), 15 (btm bkgd); Mike Elliott, 12 (nest); Muhammad Desta Laksana, 2–3; Okuneva, Back Cover (bkgd), 3, 12 (bkgd), 21 (bkgd); Olena Boiko, 15 (top griffin); olllikeballoon, 12 (tub); opicobello, 8 (marker strokes, tear), 10 (tear); PARFENOV1976, 6–7; Pasko Maksim, Back Cover (tear), 23 (tear), 24 (tear); pitju, 7 (page curl), 10 (page curl), 21 (page curl); Planet Urf, 18–19 (griffin); Ron Dale, 5 (marker stroke), 6 (marker stroke), 13, 20 (marker stroke); Sararoom Design, 15 (book); totallypic, 20 (arrow); Yevgen Kravchenko, 1 (brush), 12 (brush); your, 18–19 (clouds) Every effort has been made to contact copyright holders for material reproduced in this book. Any omissions will be rectified in subsequent printings if notice is given to the publisher.

contents

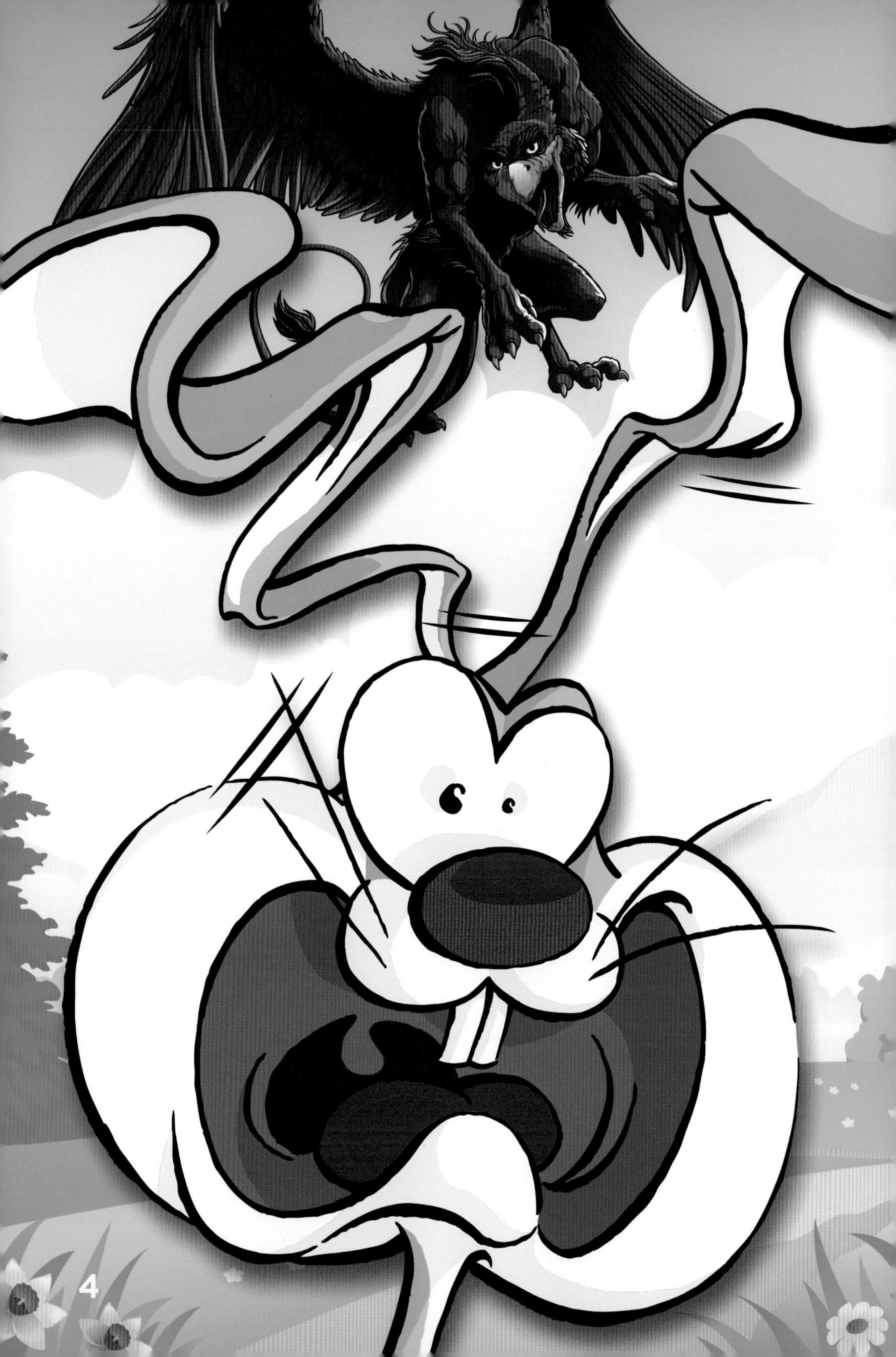

Chapter 1

Is a Griffin Right for You?

A griffin flies through the air on large wings. With a screech, it dives down to catch a rabbit. Its **talons** close around the fluffy creature with a crunch. The griffin then flies off. The rabbit will make a great gift for its owner.

Griffins are powerful creatures. And they make incredible pets. Just imagine waking up to its eagle scream in the morning! Owning a griffin isn't all fun and games, though. They need special care.

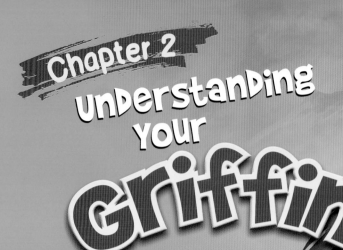

Chapter 2
Understanding Your Griffin

Before bringing home a griffin, you must know all about it. Griffins are part lion and part eagle. They have lionlike bodies and back legs. Their wings, heads, and talons are those of eagles.

Griffins are very smart. They're always flying around, looking for information. Griffins believe knowledge makes them strong.

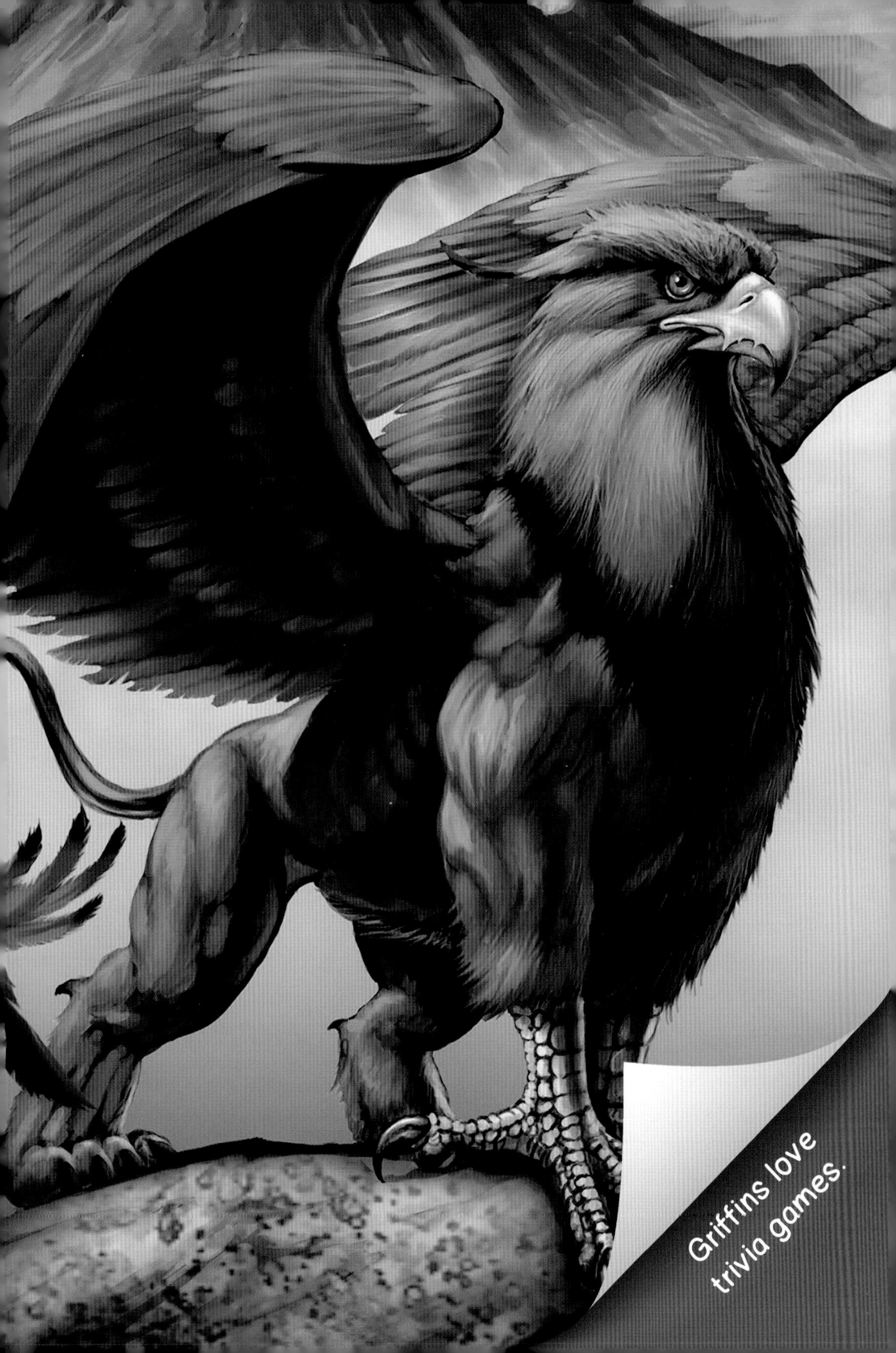
Griffins love
trivia games.

Also like cats, griffins need their space. Be sure to give yours plenty of alone time.

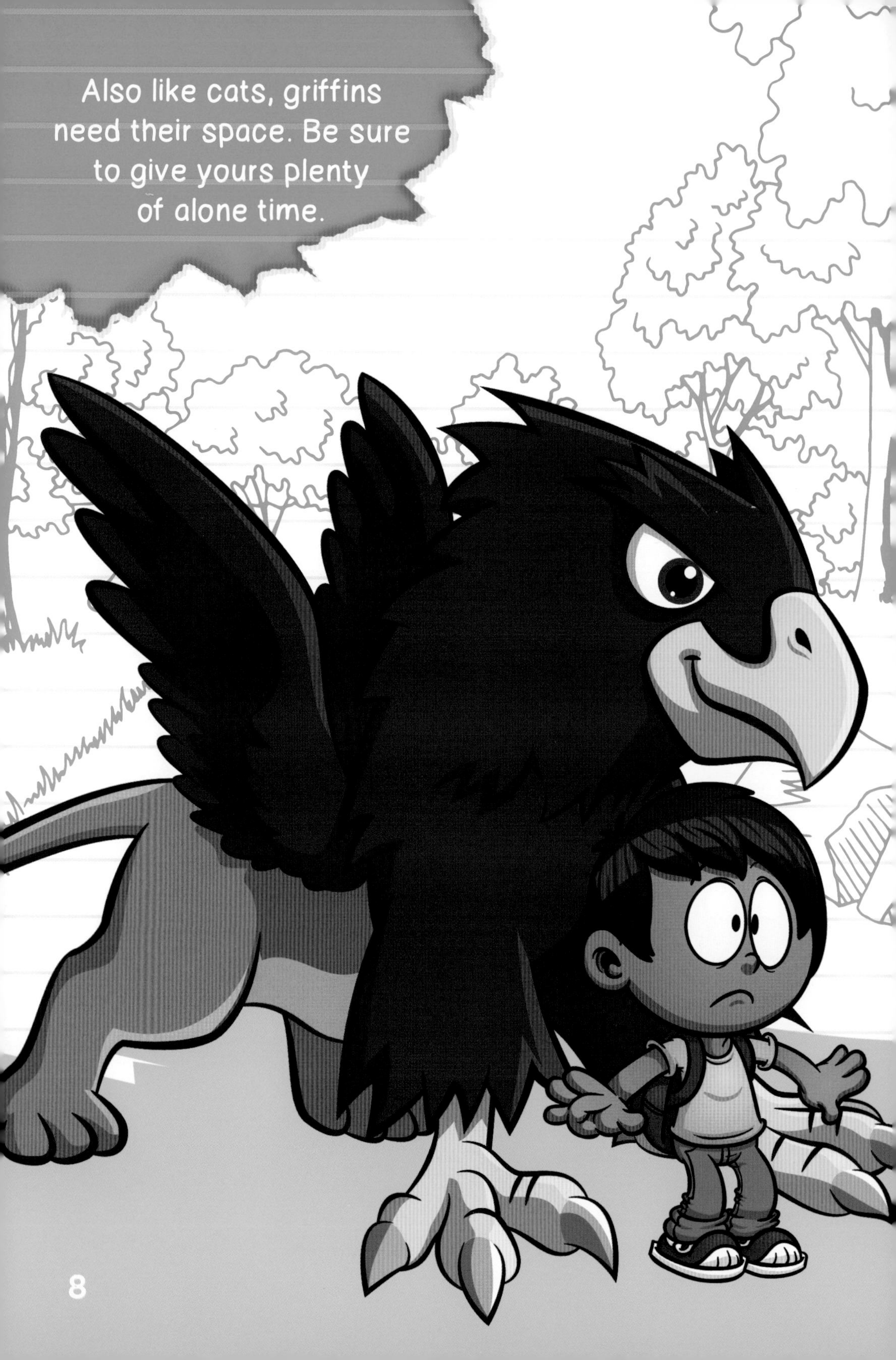

Loyal Pets

Griffins are incredibly **loyal** creatures. In stories, griffins stick up for their families and friends. Your griffin will stick up for you too. It'll come to love you. Your griffin might not always show it, though. Don't worry! That's just its **feline** instincts kicking in. Just like cats, griffins can act a bit stuck up.

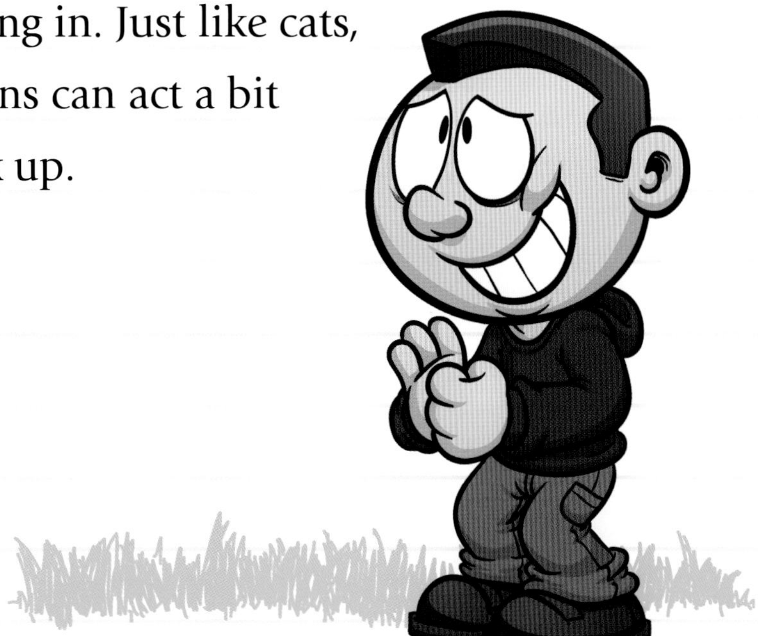

Strong Fighters

These animals are also powerful fighters. One **legend** says they're stronger than eight lions and 100 eagles. Griffins are known to carry **prey** high in the air. Then the griffins drop it. Splat! Remember these facts, and keep an eye on your griffin. Don't let it near other pets. Your neighbors do not want their pets splattered.

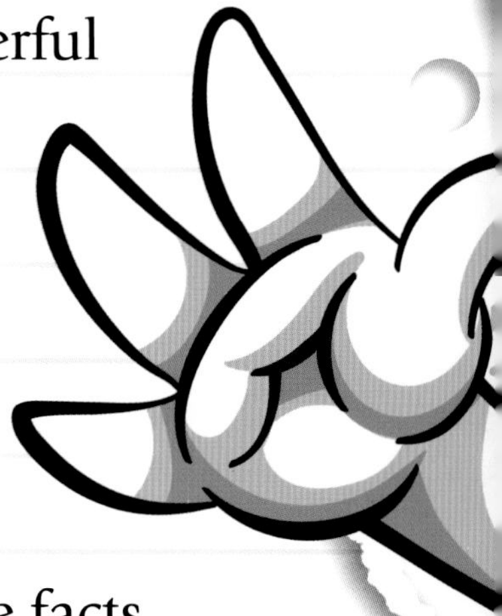

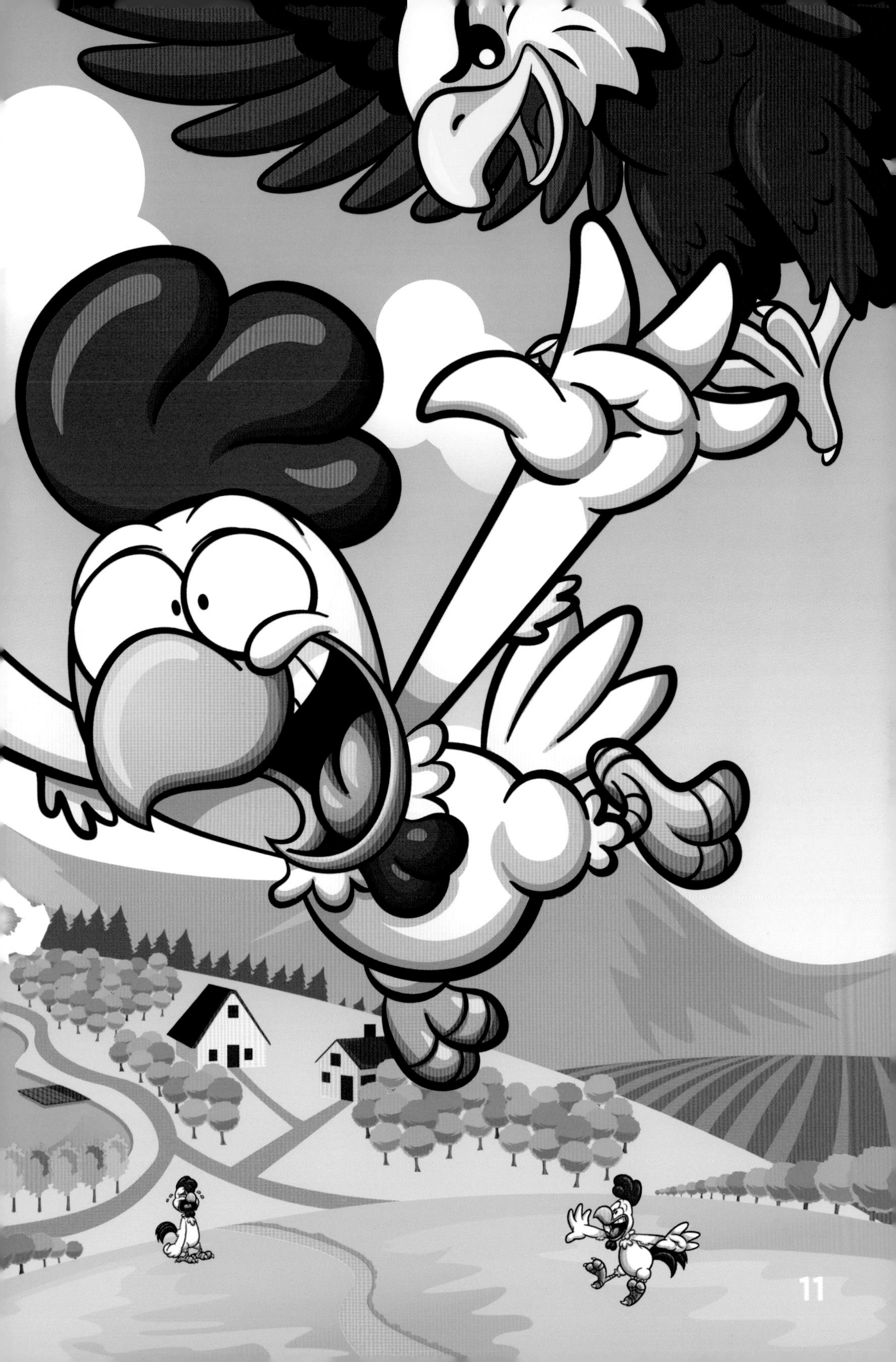

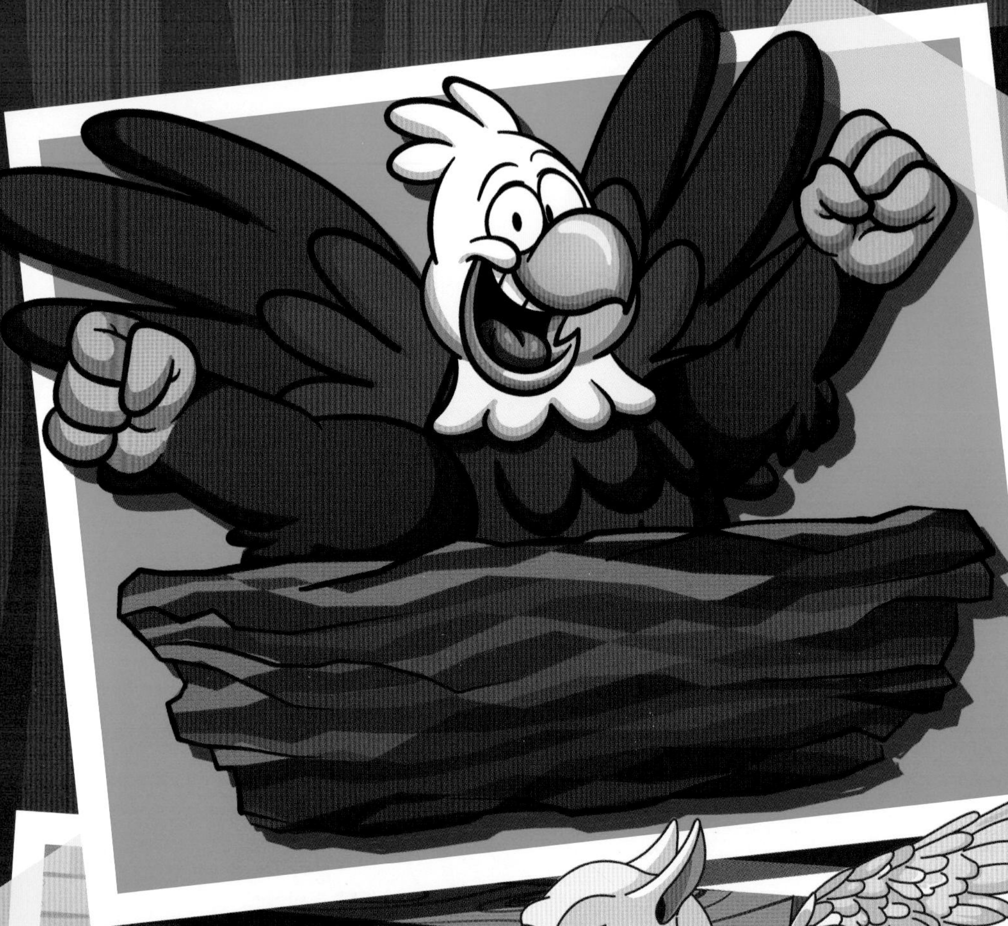
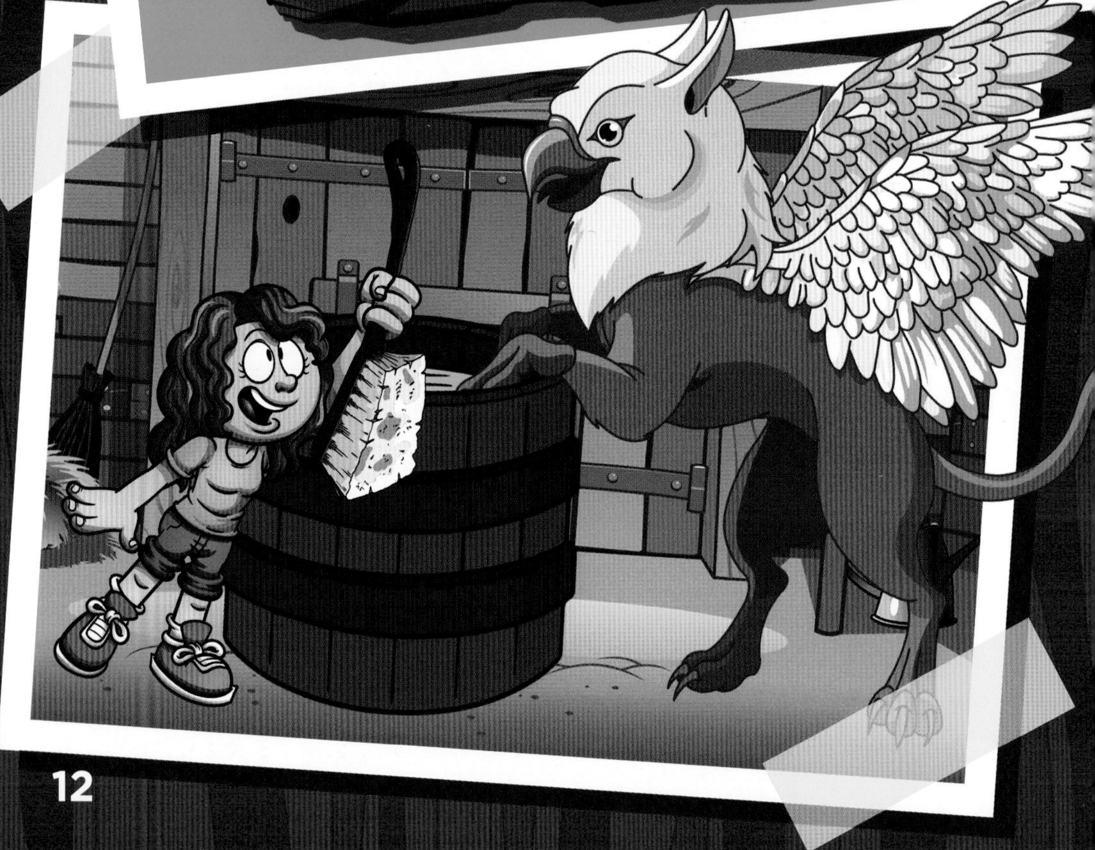

Chapter 3
Caring for Your Griffin

Griffin care can be confusing. You might wonder if your pet likes a nest or a cat bed. The answer is bed. But decorate it with twigs and branches.

Many people ask about grooming too. Being part lion, the griffin wants to lick itself clean. But its eagle beak makes licking very hard. Give your griffin a long-handled brush and water. It'll grab the brush and scrub itself.

Griffins can become the size of a large horse. Odds are, it'll get too big for your house. You'll need to keep yours in a garage or shed.

Exercise and Play

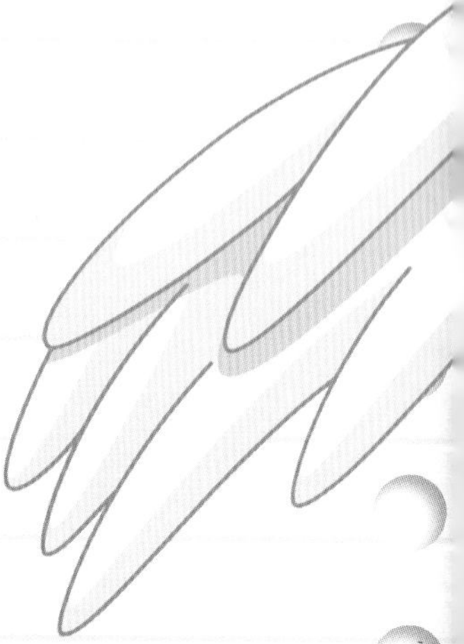

Griffins need lots of space to run around. You'll want to have a large yard or live near a park. Griffins also love to stretch their wings and fly. They need at least two hours of flying a day.

Griffins also love to learn. Be a good owner, and take your pet to the library. Go to museums too. Just make sure to keep your griffin on a leash.

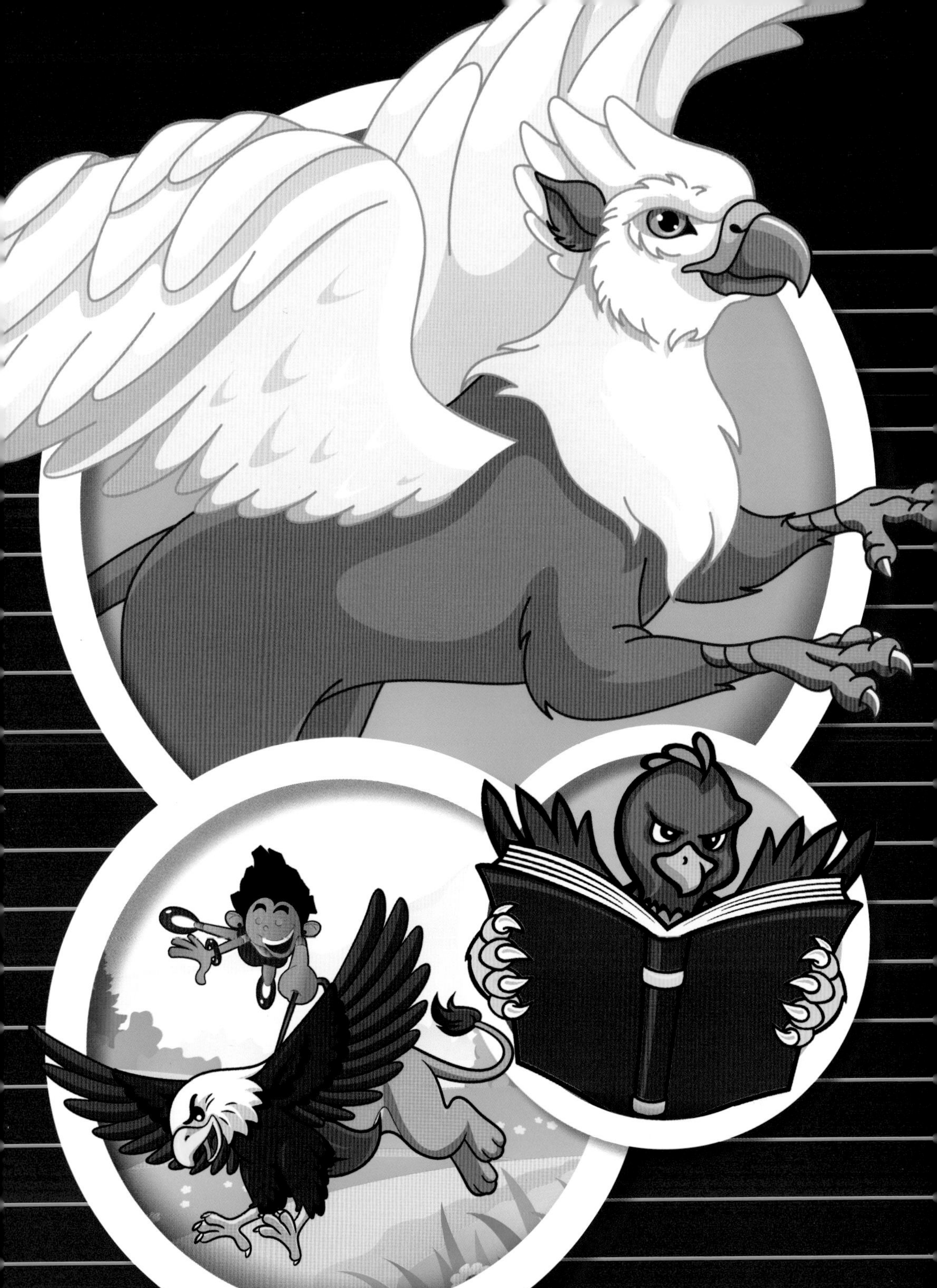

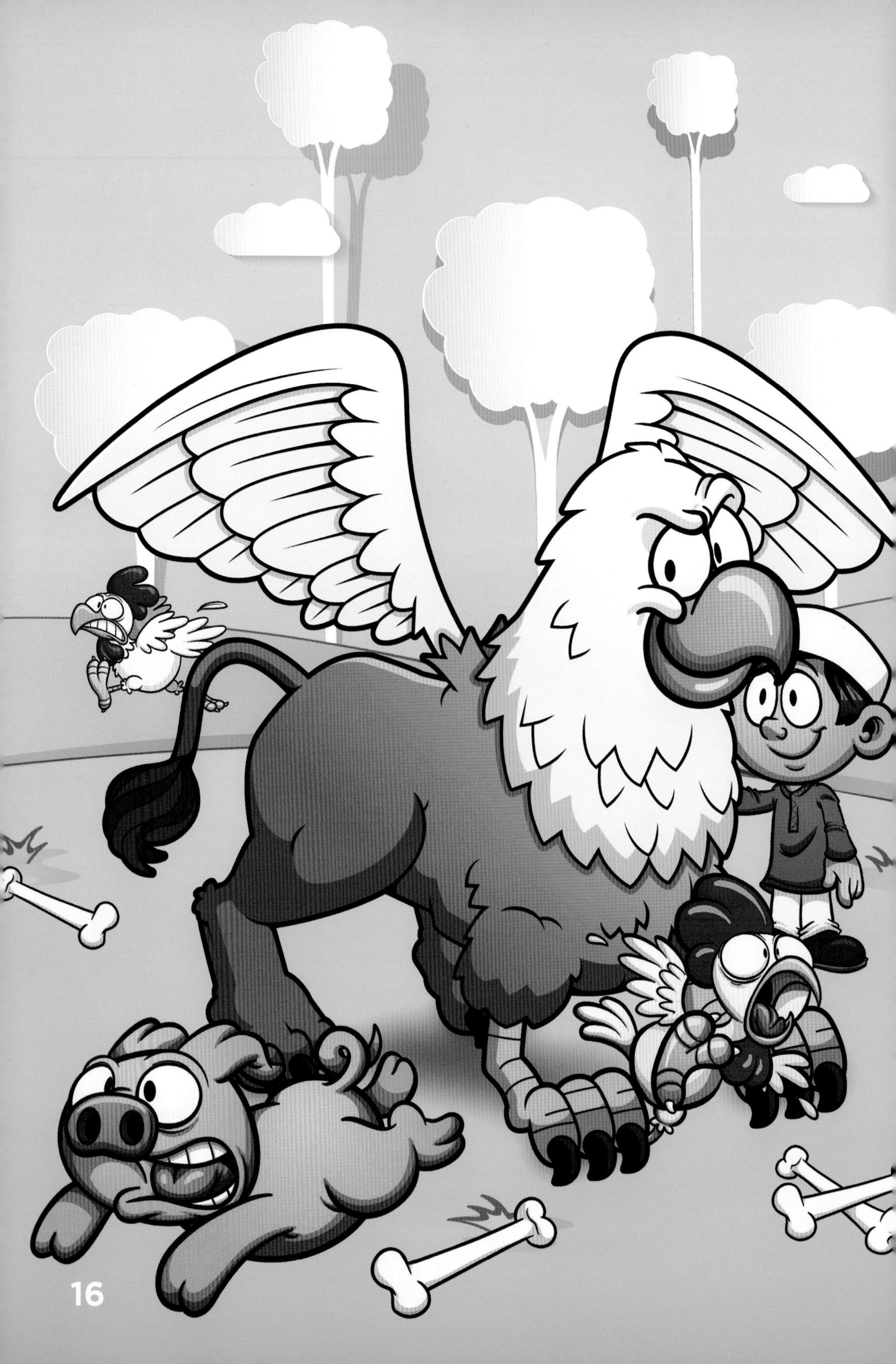

Hunting and Eating

Eagles and lions are both fierce **predators**. So it's no surprise that griffins eat meat. But you can't just feed them meat. Griffins need to hunt. You'll need to bring live animals to your home. Try chickens when your griffin is young. As your pet grows, it'll need bigger prey. Small ponies are a good choice.

Griffins are messy eaters. They often leave blood and bones behind. You'll have to be OK with cleaning gross messes.

A Lifelong Friend

Griffins aren't the easiest pets to own. They're messy and need special care. Feeding them can be expensive too. But they are also a lot of fun. Treat your griffin well, and you'll have a long friendship.

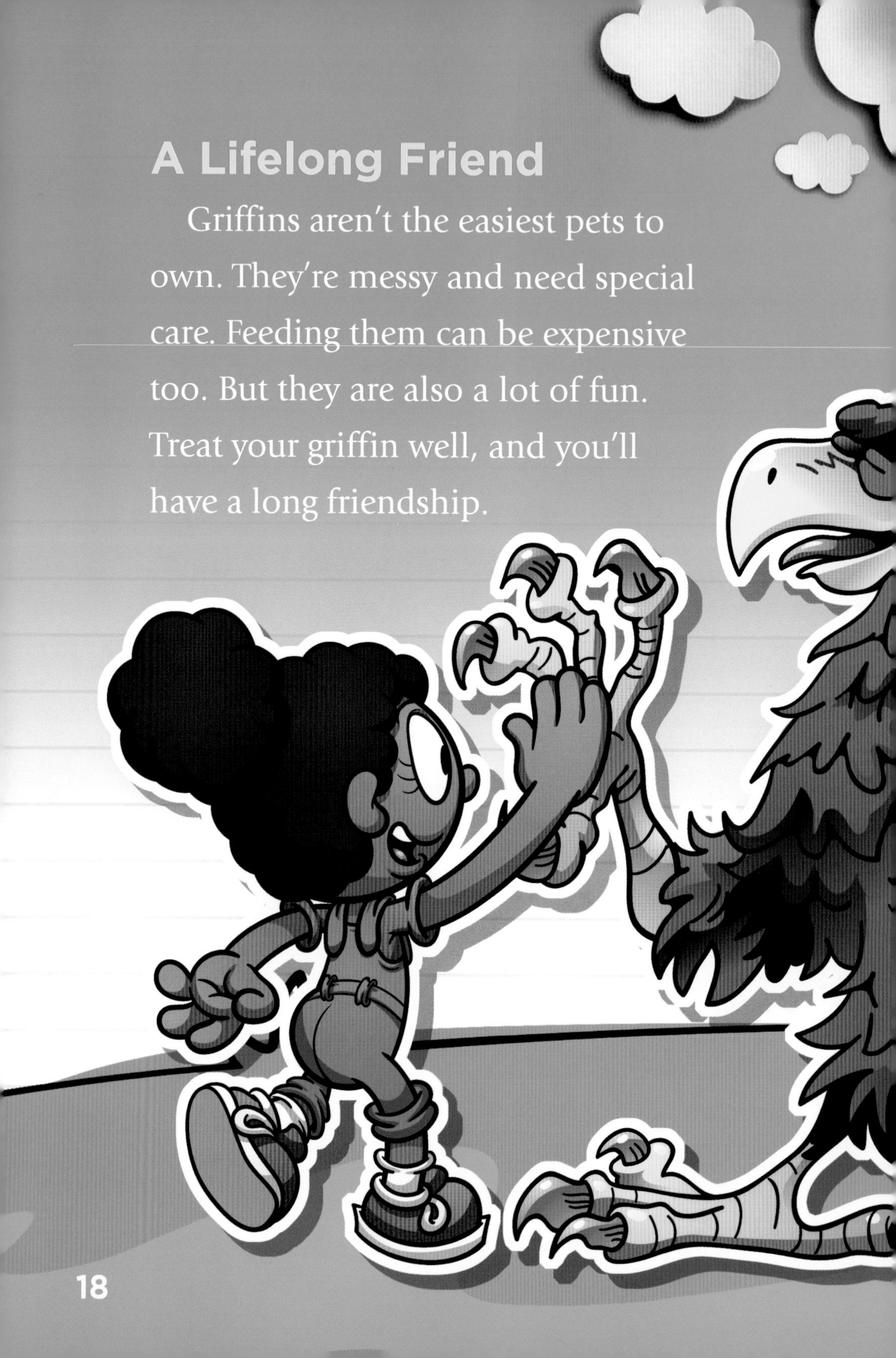

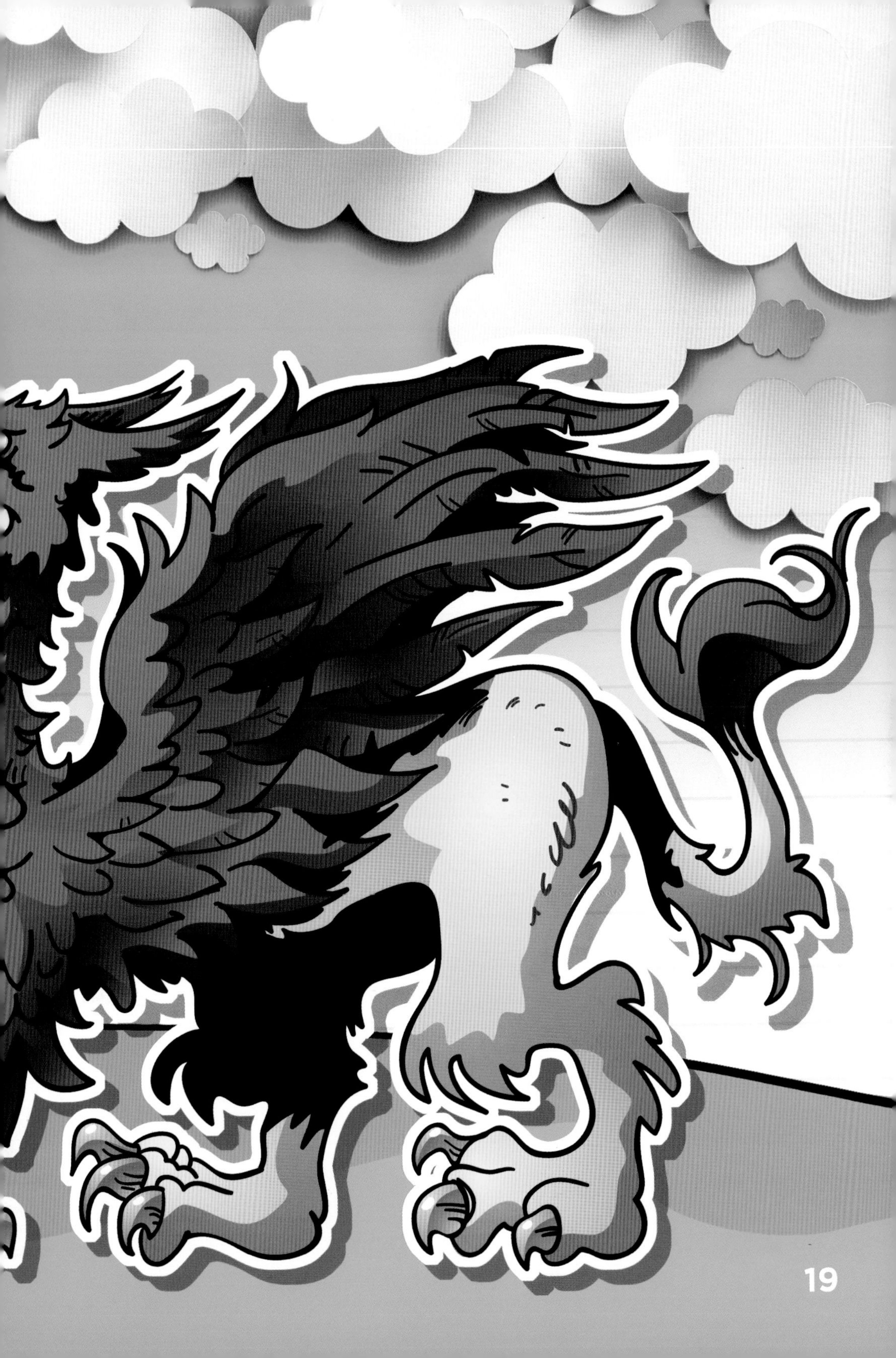

Chapter 4

Get in on the

Hi Jinx

Griffins aren't real. But people have told stories about them for thousands of years. **Ancient** people found bones that confused them. The bones looked like they came from a lion-bird creature. They were actually from dinosaurs. But ancient people didn't know about dinosaurs. So they probably made up the griffin. Just imagine what life would be like if griffins were real!

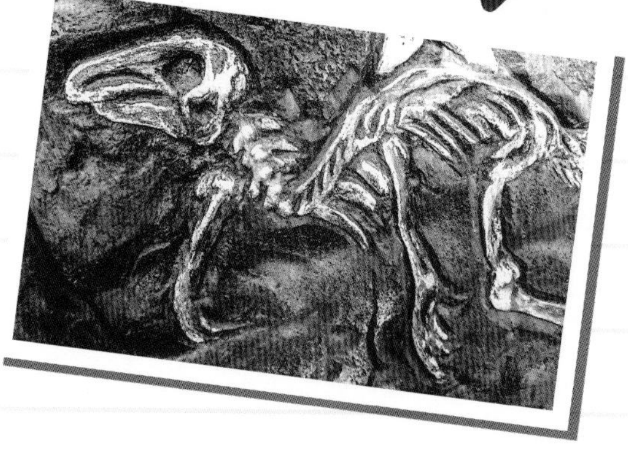

Take It One Step More

1. Do you think a very smart creature would be happy living as a pet? Why or why not?

2. Many people enjoy stories about magical or made-up creatures. Why do you think that is?

3. Make up your own **hybrid** animal. What does it look like? What kind of traits does it have?

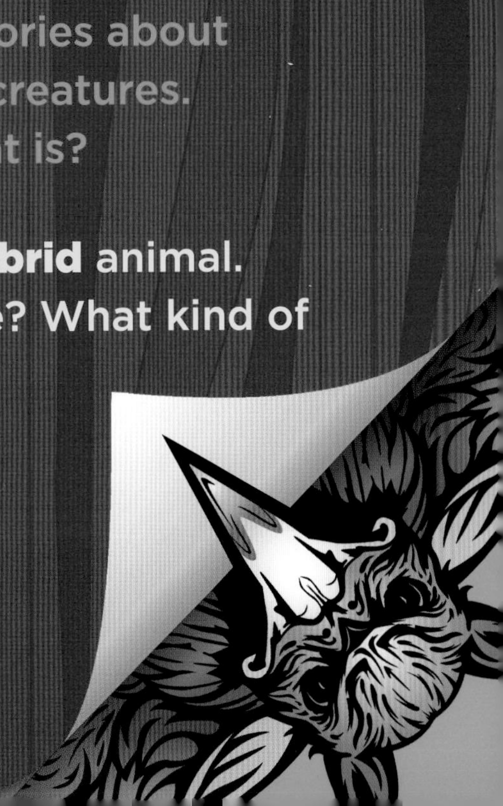

GLOSSARY

ancient (AYN-shunt)—from a time long ago

feline (FEE-lahyn)—of or relating to the cat family

hybrid (HAHY-brid)—of mixed origin

legend (LEJ-uhnd)—a story from the past that cannot be proven true

loyal (LOY-uhl)—having complete support for someone or something

predator (PRED-uh-tuhr)—an animal that eats other animals

prey (PRAY)—an animal hunted or killed for food

talon (TAH-luhn)—one of the sharp claws on the feet of some birds

LEARN MORE

BOOKS

Holland, Simon. *Magnificent Magical Beasts: Inside Their Secret World.* New York: Bloomsbury, 2016.

Loh-Hagan, Virginia. *Griffins.* Magic, Myth, and Mystery. Ann Arbor, MI: Cherry Lake Publishing, 2018.

Marsico, Katie. *Beastly Monsters: From Dragons to Griffins.* Monster Mania. Minneapolis: Lerner Publications, 2017.

WEBSITES

Ancient Greece for Kids: Monsters and Creatures of Greek Mythology
www.ducksters.com/history/ancient_greece/monsters_and_creatures_of_greek_mythology.php

Griffin
kids.britannica.com/kids/article/griffin/390038

Griffin: World Mythology
www.kidzworld.com/article/1932-greek-mythology-griffin

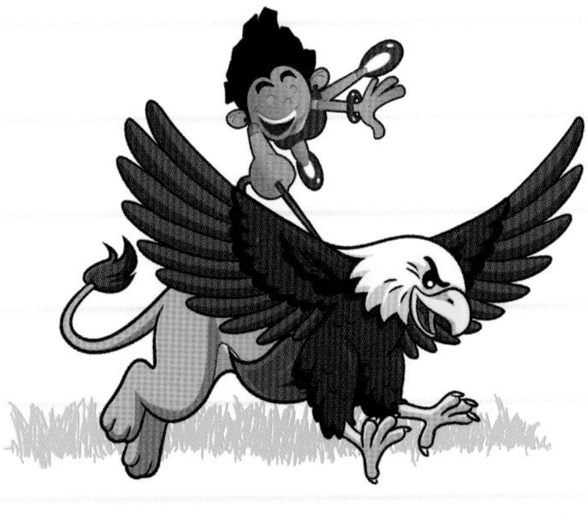

INDEX